PUFFIN BOOKS

Daughter of the Sea

Berlie Doherty is a distinguished writer for young people,
twice winner of the prestigious Carnegie Medal. A former
teacher, she has worked in schools broadcasting and adult
education. This is her sixth book published by Penguin
Children's Books. She has also written for adults and for
radio as well as the theatre. Berlie Doherty lives in the Peak
District.

D0337308

Other books by Berlie Doherty

DEAR NOBODY

THE SNAKE STONE

Berlie Doherty

Daughter of the Sea

Illustrated by Sîan Bailey

PUFFIN BOOKS

PUFFIN BOOKS

Published by the Penguin Group
Penguin Books Ltd, 27 Wrights Lane, London W8 5TZ, England
Penguin Putnam Inc., 375 Hudson Street, New York, New York 10014, USA
Penguin Books Australia Ltd, Ringwood, Victoria, Australia
Penguin Books Canada Ltd, 10 Alcorn Avenue, Toronto, Ontario, Canada M4V 3B2
Penguin Books (NZ) Ltd, 182–190 Wairau Road, Auckland 10, New Zealand

Penguin Books Ltd, Registered Offices: Harmondsworth, Middlesex, England

First published by Hamish Hamilton Ltd 1996
Published in Puffin Books 1998
1 3 5 7 9 10 8 6 4 2

Text copyright © Berlie Doherty, 1996
Illustrations copyright © Sian Bailey, 1996
All rights reserved

The moral right of the author and illustrator has been asserted

Filmset in Bembo

Made and printed in England by Clays Ltd, St Ives plc

British Library Cataloguing in Publication Data
A CIP catalogue record for this book is available from the British Library

ISBN 0–140–37951–7

To my daughters
Janna and Sally

Contents

My tale is of the sea. It takes place in the far north, where ice has broken land into jagged rocks, and where black and fierce tides wash the shores. Hail is flung far on lashing winds, and winters are long and dark. Men haunt the sea, and the sea gives up to them a glittering harvest. And it is said that the people of the sea haunt the land.

My tale is of the daughter of the sea. The best way to hear the tale is to creep into the lee of the rocks when the herring boats have just landed. The gulls will be keening around you. The women hone knives on the stones, and their hands will be brown from the wind and the fish-gut slime. And as they work they talk to each other of things they've always known.

That's when the story's told.

Imagine a woman called Jannet, standing on the weed-wet stones. It would be dark, and the spray would be scraping her cheeks and the wind would be delving into her hair. She would be looking into the damsony dark and seeing nothing. And imagine her husband, Munroe Jaffray, crouching into his boat with the wild waves lumbering round him. And there's another to think of. Eilean o da Freya. Some say she's as weak in the head as a stunned herring. Others say she has the wisdom of the ancients. Jannet, Munroe, and Eilean. They're the ones who know for sure what happened on the night of the freak storm.

This is the tale.

1

The Freak Storm

Jannet Jaffray had gone to bed early and woke to the sound of a wild kind of wailing, far out and away at sea. It faded as soon as she sat up to listen. She lay in the dark hearing only the waves and the wind and this shadow of singing, and then put out her fingers to touch her husband's arm. With a missing beat of her heart she knew that Munroe was not home.

In minutes she was down on the shore, her lantern high in her hand, and counting the fishing boats that had been beached up by the rocks. As her lamp guttered its last breath she had counted all home except for Munroe's. The sea was high and frenzied; the moon was a ghost face, hiding and squinting as the dark clouds rolled.

'Munroe!' she called uselessly. It was on nights like this that the sea snatched lives instead of yielding fish. Jannet heard footsteps treading the sand behind her, and turned, smiling, expecting it to be her husband come home safe to her from another bay along the coast. There was no one to be seen. Yet again she heard footsteps in the shadows.

'Are you there?'

Nothing to hear or see.

'Then is it Eilean?'

She was answered this time by low singing coming like nightmares out of the huddled rocks. She knew the sound well.

'Go home, Eilean. There's nothing for you here.'

The woman Eilean edged closer, wet skirt clinging and hair like weeds round her face. She often came down to the shore on nights like this. It was as if she was searching for something that could never be found. She stood by Jannet's side, saying nothing.

Jannet stared out into the foam-flecked mouths of the waves. Munroe was somewhere there, and she would not be going home herself until she had sight of him.

Munroe was not far away. His boat was caught between the dangerous rocks of the skerries. He knew he must wait till first light before he tried to pull clear. The night had begun with a calm sea, though the fishing had not been good. He was about to turn for home when he heard a strange keening on the wind, swelling and fading like the flow of the tide itself. He saw that the water beneath his boat flashed with a streaming shoal of fishes. He followed it, leaning out in his eagerness to pull in the catch.

That was when the storm had risen out of nowhere. Waves snapped around him like a pack of wild dogs, forcing him into the ring of rocks for shelter. He was safe enough there. Just outside the skerries there was a wild frenzy of waves that would toss his boat like a shell.

Black clouds billowed across the sky. The moonlight came through in flashes, giving him brief glimpses of the waves and the tower of the spray. No going home yet, he thought.

It was in one of these moon flashes that he saw the child in the water.

It could be that Jannet fell asleep standing up that night, with the wind holding her round like ropes as she swayed. She didn't know that the tide had dropped or the sky was bleaching to grey until a voice called out to her: 'Jannet!' And there he was, riding high through the sea-mist – Munroe, her husband, safe home, and the small boat all in one piece. She ran knee-deep into the water to haul the boat in, and Munroe jumped out to help her.

'Why were you out there in this weather?' she shouted, the wind tearing her voice this way and that. He did not hear her, and she did not repeat it. He was safe, after all.

'I've a fine catch for you,' he told her. He reached back into his boat for the basket he used for carrying small fry. 'I'll show you when we get home.'

And just as they were leaving, with the boat pulled up on high sand and lashed to boulders, Eilean crept out of her shelter of rocks.

'I forgot about her!' Jannet whispered. 'She's been idling here all night waiting for your corpse to be washed ashore!'

The woman scuttled over to them, more like a crab than anything, the way she picked over the sharp pebbles. She tried to grab at the basket but Munroe swung it up away from her, holding it high above her head.

'Not for you!' he warned.

'What is it you have in there?' she asked him. 'A fish that sings. Is that it?'

2
The Child

Home, and the fire nearly dead in the hearth. Jannet raked through the peat embers and blew life back into them. Munroe put his basket down and lifted the sacking rag he had draped across it. He held the lantern over it. Then he replaced the rag carefully and went to squat by his wife where she knelt on the floor.

'Jannet,' he said. 'What is it you want most in the world?'

She laughed a little, pushing him away from her and pouting. 'I have it, don't I? A husband home safe from the sea.'

'No, that was what you wanted last night, because of the storm. But before that, what did you want?'

'Don't tease me, Munroe. You must know how weary I am.'

'Since we met, Jannet. What is it we've always wanted since we first married?'

Jannet looked away from him and into the purring flames. She saw herself again as a young girl, and Munroe a red-haired boy of eighteen. They were standing on the hill looking down on the scattering of humped croft houses and the coloured boats in the bay. Above them the curlew bubbled its keening liquid cry, that gripped your heart to hear it, and Munroe had said, 'I don't ever want to leave this place.'

'Why should you ever leave it?' Jannet had asked, startled by his remark and by the rush of dismay it had brought to her.

'Say I wanted to marry someone, and she didn't want me. I should have to leave then, shouldn't I?'

He had laughed, and Jannet understood by his laughter what his clumsy words were really saying. She crept a shy hand into his and said simply, 'When I have a child, it will be yours, Munroe.'

They married that year, and in all those thirty years since that day they remained childless.

Nowadays they never spoke of it. It was a hurtful thing, for all that, to see the handful of crofters' children at play, and not to have a child of their own among them.

'Say what it is we've always wanted,' Munroe urged her again.

Jannet shook her head. He stood up then and brought the basket over to where they could see it, in the glow of the fire. His breathing was not steady. He took away the sacking that draped over his basket and Jannet peered inside it.

'A baby!' she gasped. 'A dead baby!'

'No. Not dead. Feel her. She's sleeping, and warm.'

Hardly daring to let out her breath, Jannet touched the baby's cheek. She stared at her husband.

'And you fished her out of the sea!'

'Round by the skerry rocks, where I've spent most of the night. I heard something strange, and followed it in. And that's where I found her, in the water. The sea was too wild to chance moving. So I kept low, with the bairn sleeping all this time in the basket. I kept touching her. I kept thinking any minute she must die, fished out like that from a bitter storm. But she slept on, sweet as dreams.

She's ours, Jannet. She's a gift from the sea.'

Jannet put her hands over her face. 'What are you saying! A gift from the sea!' The thoughts in her head were stripped raw. How many times had she stood at the brim of the bay and spoken her wishes out loud, 'Please, please, send me a child,' when only the gulls could have heard her? How many times, she wondered, had Munroe spoken the same words, out there on the tide?

'Perhaps she was from a wrecked boat?' she asked.

'There was nothing to see. There she was, floating in the weeds, and here she is, in our house! She's ours now.' He bent down, crooking his finger to brush the baby's cheek. He was already used to her. He already thought of her as his daughter. Jannet could see that.

'Pick her up, why don't you? Hold her.'

'I couldn't. She doesn't seem real, Munroe. If her people come for her . . .'

'They won't.'

The baby stirred in her sleep, seeking round as if for food. Her fingers flexed and closed again. Munroe lifted her out of the basket. He was a big man, and the baby looked tiny in his cupped hands. Jannet felt her old longing stirring within her.

'It's cruel of you to bring her here, only to have her taken away again!'

'No one will take her away. Why should they?'

'Did she have nothing with her?' Jannet looked into the smoke swirling up from the peat, as if she were trying to picture there what Munroe had seen. He kept quiet. He thought back to the silver-black pool, the odd pale bobbing shape, his fear as he leaned over the side of the boat, the touch of a child in his hands. As he lifted her out of the water he had felt something slip away, like a rag of soft skin. He knew what it was, and he had let it go. He had borne her up and warmed life into her, wrapped her in sacking, cradled her to him. By the time the moonlight showed again there was nothing to see on the water. He told Jannet nothing of this.

'She wants feeding,' he said. 'Look how she's hunting round. Take her.'

He put her into Jannet's arms. Scared, she looked up at Munroe. 'How can I feed her?' she whispered. 'How can a barren woman like me give her milk?' But she could hardly bear the softness of the baby's skin, or the mewing sounds she made, or the way her head twisted against her, searching for milk. She put the baby's mouth to her breast. 'Just to try it,' she said. 'Just to know how it feels.'

And she was half swooning then with the power that had come to her. The baby sucked, yes, and Jannet's milk flowed. Call it magic or miracle, but that was what happened the morning after the storm.

'See? She's ours,' said Munroe.

For a second the baby fluttered open her eyes. They were the colour of oceans.

If Munroe and his wife had looked out of their door at that moment they would have seen Eilean leaving the upturned boat that was her home. She led her pony down to the bay. The tide was ebbing, and this was the time for bringing in the pots of crabs from the cliff caves. Her baskets were tied to the pony's flanks, but she left him chewing seaweed on the shore. She dragged her own small boat down to the water and rowed out as far as the skerries, where Munroe had found shelter in the night. Basking seals slithered down to the sea as she drew near. The rocks were blue with mussel shells. Eilean lifted a small pail from inside the boat and hooked it over her arm. Then she climbed out.

On her hands and knees, scraping her pail, Eilean clambered from rock to rock. Green slippery weed trailed like strands of hair. She lay flat on her belly with her hands dipping into the pools that the tide had left, as if she were trawling for a precious catch. Crabs sidled out of her grasp, but it was not crabs that she was hunting that day.

And at last she found what she searched for. She brought it up out of the pool with the sea streaming from it and held it up towards the pale sun. It gleamed like white silk.

She bent down and scooped her pail into the rock pool, pulling away bits of moss and weeds, digging down for shells. Then she slid into it the gift she had found, the mantle that had slipped like a skin from the daughter of the sea.

Next morning Jannet walked out as calm as you please with her kishie basket slung over her back. She might have been carrying linen to wash in the burn. This time she had her baby, tucked down away from the wind. She climbed the grassy hill to the cluster of houses where most of the islanders lived. The first house belonged to old Mary, her mother. Geese and ducks came squawking towards her as she approached the door.

'Is that Jannet?' her mother called.

'It is,' said Jannet. 'And I've something to tell you.'

Old Mary put down her knitting and came out to the light. Jannet lowered the basket to the ground.

'I had a baby last night,' she said.

Her mother stood in the doorway as if she had been struck by a spell. 'It's not possible,' she said at last, shaking life back into her head.

But Jannet lifted the baby out of the basket and put her in her mother's arms.

'What madness is this?' Mary demanded. 'And not a word to any of us?' She tucked her hair that was the colour of grain inside her bonnet and peered down at the bundle. 'Sure she's a beauty!' she crooned. 'Skin like pearls.' She looked up again and her hazy eyes searched Jannet's face. 'There might be a family likeness there.'

Jannet smiled.

Mary looked at her own hands, leathery brown from the sun and the salty wind. 'Look at what the years do to us! You were as silky as a little mackerel yourself, Jannet, when you were a bairn.'

The last of the houses, just over the stepping-stones, was where Jannet's sister Morag lived. Jannet and her mother went there together, with the baby asleep again on Jannet's back.

Morag screwed up her eyes as though the morning sun was blinding her and looked from the baby to Jannet and from Jannet to the baby, shaking her head. 'This is not your child.' She was older than Jannet, and had always been right in everything. She had four sons herself, and with every one of them she had been as round as a berry for months on end. 'I'd have known.'

'Then whose is it?' Jannet demanded. 'I never left the croft yesterday, except to meet Munroe from the boat. Did you see me leave?'

Well, that was true. Morag lived at the last croft before the ferry. Nobody passed her house without her yelling a greeting to them, asking where they were off to and what they were buying and when they expected to be home. Jannet would have had to crawl on her hands and knees to get past Morag's door without being seen.

The baby began to hiccup for food. Saying nothing, Jannet unbuttoned her dress and put the child to her breast. Her milk flowed to the baby's clutch and suck. She looked up at her sister, her eyes dreamy and smiling. Old Mary clucked like a hen, and Morag was silenced at last.

After that word got round on the wind that Jannet and Munroe were parents. The women came round to marvel and the men to tease, and the children came shy and tiptoeing. The house was crowded with people from all over the island. They sat on the benches and the floor and told each other stories of their own babies. Outside, the wind was moaning and whistling, and the lemony sun turned to grey dusk.

The baby lay in the basket with her fingers grasping the air as though it was made of ropes and hanging reeds. Every now and again she would open her sea-dark eyes and stare round her. She seemed to take in everything – the smiling faces around her, the flickering light of the fire, the shadows on the crack-crazed walls; the gleam of salted fish strung from the beams, sunshine coming hazy through the door.

'I swear she can see us!' Jannet whispered.

'Too young!' Morag insisted, before Munroe had a chance to agree with his wife. But it was true. The baby had such a calm steady look. She seemed to absorb the detail of everything she looked at.

'We must have a christening feast,' old Mary said. 'When did we last have a party on the island?'

'And this is a real occasion,' Munroe's mother Margaret agreed. 'My Munroe and Jannet parents at last, with grey hairs in their heads, both of them! It's a gift child, this is!' She picked up the baby in her old, flecked hands and dandled her on her knee. Over her head Munroe and Jannet exchanged glances and said nothing. 'Just look at the shine on her skin and her little nails! Like pearls.'

'Tam will play fiddle, and I will bake cakes,' said Morag.

'Morag will organize it,' Mary agreed.

'Scones and cheese tarts will do. It's not a wedding,' Morag went on. 'And rhubarb punch. We'll be having it on Sunday morning, straight after the christening. But yes, we have to welcome the bairn.' She folded her arms. 'Whoever she is.'

'I remember a story,' said Grandfather Jaffray suddenly from his dark corner at the back of the room, and everybody fell silent. 'Told to me years ago. A woman from over the water brought home a child from the snow.'

'When the snows come, that's a quiet time,' old Mary said. 'I do love the quiet of the snow.'

'Over there, over the water, this is what I am telling you about. And there was a child lying in the snow. About the age of young Harris.'

Morag's youngest son, leaning over the basket where the baby lay, lowered his head and smiled. 'I'll be six, won't I, Mam?' he whispered at the mention of his name.

Grandfather Jaffray cleared his throat. His mouth was a little hole in the smoky waterfall of his moustache and beard. 'Everyone came to look at the child in the snow. It was a perfect child. White and still. And the woman who found her first, wanted her.'

'She had none of her own,' said Margaret, who thought now that she'd heard the tale from the ferryman's wife.

'She had none of her own, and she lived alone.' Grandfather Jaffray began to cough. Someone passed him a mug of ale, and he drank from it slowly. Nobody in the room moved or spoke, all waiting to hear the tale of the child in the snow.

'"She's no use to you," the woman was told.' He passed the mug back. 'But she carried the child into the house when the night was dark. She put her by the fire, and listened out for her breathing to start, so she would know that the child had woken up. Will you give me a drop more of that ale, Jannet?'

His long silence while the ale was drunk was more than Harris could bear. He shuffled over on his knees to the old man and tugged at his trouser leg. 'And did she wake up?'

'The woman had to wait until morning came, and she fell asleep herself with waiting. And it was a sound that woke her up.' He keened softly in the back of his throat.

'The child crying!' said Harris.

'No, it was not the child crying, though it sounded like crying.' The old man stood up and shuffled over to where the peat fire blazed in the middle of the room. He tipped the dregs of his mug on to it. The fire whined like a baby. 'That was the sound the woman heard. She opened her eyes, and saw a pool of water where the child had been lying next to the fire. Well, the woman went outside sobbing, thinking the child had woken up and gone out again into the snow, and the pool was where she'd been lying. And that might be what happened.'

'But it wasn't?' prompted Harris.

'No, it wasn't,' agreed Grandfather Jaffray. 'What happened was this. The child was a child of snow, and the love of that woman had caused her to melt away.'

There was a sigh of agreement in the room.

'It wasn't meant for her, you see,' he said.

'I remember that story,' said Mary.

'And is it true?' Harris asked, back at the basket now and dandling his fingers against the baby's cheek.

'All stories are true,' said the old man. He stood up to go and the people in the room made a passageway for him to shuffle through. Jannet put her arm under his elbow to steady his way to the door.

'Why did you tell us that story?' she asked him, dry in her throat.

'I don't know,' he said. 'I don't know why I remembered that tonight.'

The sun had gone. Mary and Margaret joined the old man.

'The light's going fast,' Mary called.

Harris ran after them and soon afterwards the other crofters left, guiding each other with calls and whistles over the dark windy hills to their homes.

When all the visitors had gone and they were alone again, Munroe rocking the baby in his big hands and chuckling down at her, Jannet went to the door and stood outside, leaning against the wall. The wind had dropped with the turn of the tide. She could hear the soft sea breathing. The sky looked like a field scattered with flowers.

'We are blessed,' Munroe called to her.

Jannet didn't turn back to him. She thought of the deep ocean, and the shells rocking on its bed. She thought of the fishes slipping through the dark waters; and, out on the sandbanks, the grey seals.

'I'm afraid of losing her,' she said, but low, so Munroe wouldn't hear and be hurt. She could just see the shape of a woman going down to the rocks. It would be Eilean, gone out to watch the water again. Jannet closed the door and went to sit by her husband, letting the baby's small hand grasp her finger. Joy and sorrow surged in her. Her throat ached. This was the child she'd always wanted.

'If she's to be christened on Sunday we'll have to name her,' Munroe said. 'Should it be Mary or Jannet?'

'You saved her from the sea that night.' Jannet stroked the child's gleaming cheek. 'And she saved you.'

'That would be true. If I hadn't heard that crying sound I would never have gone into the skerries.'

'In my childhood there was a story. It was about a sea princess who saved a man from drowning out there on the skerries.'

'I know it. She brought him home safely to Hamna Voe.'

'And what was the name of the princess? Do you know it?'

The baby sighed, flexing her fists against the sides of her basket. At the far end of the room the cows shifted in the straw.

'I think it was Gioga,' said Munroe.

Jannet nodded. She touched her husband's hand shyly. 'Gioga. That's what I want to call her.'

3

The Christening

It was a fine blue day that Sunday, but blowy, with cloud specks like shoals of sprats chasing each other. Morag organized the placing together of tables outside the kirk, and put stones on the corners to hold down the linen cloths. In church the children sang for the baby, who smiled round in Jannet's arms. When the minister put water on her forehead she opened her eyes and laughed out loud, which made the entire congregation laugh too. He dabbled a little more on her to make her laugh again.

While the feasting was going on, and cheese tarts

and scones were being eaten, apple jelly, rhubarb punch and christening cake, little Gioga was passed from woman to woman.

'See the shine on her skin!' they all marvelled. 'And the colour of her eyes! They have all the shades of the sea in them!'

Jannet was silent. Like her husband, she had almost come to believe that Gioga was their own child. She had been with them now for five days and every minute of that time had been devoted to her. Munroe hadn't even ventured out into his boat again. If the truth were told they were both frightened to leave her side. It was almost as if they were afraid that she might disappear; as though if one or the other of them were to turn away from her basket for a moment they would look back to find it empty, and the dream would have dissolved like Grandfather Jaffray's child of snow.

'Whatever happens,' Munroe whispered to her that morning, 'we must keep our secret! For ever, mind!'

'Oh, I promise. If we tell, we lose her,' Jannet murmured. 'I'm sure of that.'

So there they were, playing the part of a real mother and father, showing off their baby with pride. It was the best day of their married lives.

After the feasting Morag's son Tam picked up his fiddle and played a slow air that he had just composed for his sweetheart, and everyone went dreamy and quiet. Then he swung into a lively jig for them all to dance.

Everyone was there. Even the crofters from the far end of the island came to wish them well. They came red-cheeked over the hill, their feet stained brown from walking through the peat bogs, and they all brought gifts. Nothing much, because none of them had much, but everyone wanted to make a special occasion of the day. Munroe's old mother Margaret pressed a silver coin in the baby's palm and chuckled as the child clutched it.

'That's your wealth,' she crooned, her breath rusty with salt. 'If I go to the grave with that much, I shall be thankful.'

Gioga gurgled up at her, and for a moment the old woman stared into the round eyes and thought she saw in them the flecks that sunlight makes on water, greeny-gold.

'Here's a necklace for her,' said Mary, dangling a coil of bright and flashing beads, laughing as Gioga dropped the coin to clutch it. 'I wore this on the day I was beautiful, when I went to be married.' She hugged her wrinkled elbows. She held the coil for a second against her own rumpled neck, then looped it round baby Gioga's. 'That's for her beauty!'

The reflected light sparkled round the child's skin. Again, old Margaret was reminded of sunlight on water, when every ripple shimmers with it.

'Well, I've brought her a bible,' said Morag. 'May she be God-fearing, clever and good.'

Grandmother Margaret jigged the baby on her knee and sang to her as the islanders joined hands and started skipping round the tables. Some of the children ran up with bunches of flowers they'd pulled from the fields – sea pinks and thrift, blue harebells, golden marsh marigolds – anxious not to be left out of the gift-giving. Munroe and Jannet danced round with the others, wildly happy that they should have a child who was the centre of everyone's attention.

It was when the feasting was at its height that Eilean shuffled up the hill from the rocks. 'The crab-woman's coming!' laughed the children. Eilean came into the ring and stood staring round at the half-eaten food, at the stools pushed aside, at the red-faced dancers. A hush fell on them, a kind of shame. No one had realized that she had not been there.

'Ah, Eilean!' said Jannet. 'I'm pleased you've come.'

'We should have sent one of the little ones down for her,' whispered Mary. 'Why didn't we think?'

'Because we didn't want her here!' Morag whispered back behind her hand. 'With her sour face!'

'There's plenty of food left,' said Munroe, in his blundering way making things worse.

'And here's a seat next to me.' Margaret patted a stool. 'Sit here, Eilean.'

'Do you think I want food?' said Eilean. 'Or dancing, or to sit and watch your sporting? I want none of them.'

She walked over to the basket where Margaret had laid the sleeping child, and she leaned right into it. Jannet ran forward with her hand to her mouth. But Eilean didn't snatch up the child. She didn't touch her. Instead she held her fists over the baby and opened them out, and down showered bladder-wrack, crabs' backs, sea shells sticky with sand, strands of dry weed.

'Never forget where you came from!' Eilean crooned to the screaming baby. 'Here's for your memory, child!'

There was a shout of outrage then as people woke from their trance of shock. Munroe scooped up the child in his arms. Old Margaret went to shake out the basket, but Jannet stopped her.

'No, leave them there,' she said. 'I want her to keep all her gifts.'

Eilean shuffled over to Jannet.

'She's not for you!' she whispered. 'And never will be. They'll want her back!'

Jannet alone heard it, and her heart went cold.

Before anyone could make sense of what Eilean had done she was running back to her upturned boat house, her feet on the shingle clapping like slow, urgent drums.

It was a strange thing, how quickly the loose clouds shawled themselves over the sun that day, and how the wind knifed up from the sea. There was nothing to hear after Eilean had gone, save for the heckle of gulls. Tam put his fiddle to his chin again and stood, bow poised.

'Shall I play on?' he asked, foolish with embarrassment.

'I'm not in the mood for dancing,' Morag said. 'Besides, it's blowing for rain. The tide has turned.'

'It would be a pity to get the food wet,' Mary agreed.

'Time for my pipe!' Old Grandfather Jaffray muttered, and stumped away back to his house, flapping his hand behind his back to show that everyone was dismissed.

The mothers called their children together. 'The bairn needs her sleep,' they said. 'Say goodbye to her and run away home.'

The children filed past Gioga's basket. They held their noses as they fingered Eilean's gift. 'Bits of seaweed!' Morag's youngest son Harris scoffed. 'Ach, she stinks!' His mother smacked him and he ran off up the hill, stuffing his fists with food, her red handmark blazing on his cheek. 'Don't care!' he shouted, his mouth bulging with bread. 'She smells like an old fish!' His brothers cast up their cries and swooped behind him, arms outstretched like wings.

Grimly Morag saw to the clearing away of food. Gulls pitched into the remains of the feast. Margaret had to be nudged awake and helped back home. Tam wrapped his fiddle in its sack and hared off after Moira, his sweetheart. And that left the mother and father, the basket of gifts and the baby.

'We know Eilean's cracked,' Munroe said. 'You mustn't take any notice of her.'

'She frightened me,' said Jannet.

'She's soft, but she can do no harm.' Munroe lifted up the baby and held her high over his head.

'Can she, wee one? We're not going to let a daft woman like that give us goose-bumps, are we? No, we're not! We've better things to do with our time.' He put Gioga into Jannet's arms and tucked the christening shawl round her. It had been Jannet's own, and Morag's before that. Grains of sand still glistened in the soft wool.

'Things like work,' Munroe went on. He picked up the basket and put his hand under Jannet's elbow. 'Tonight I go out on the sea again. I've been away long enough.'

She nodded. 'Will you go back – you know – to the skerries?'

'Where I found her? What d'you think?'

Jannet shuddered. 'I don't think you should, Munroe.'

'Then I won't. I'm curious to – but I won't, that's a promise. And you're to promise not to fret.'

'Of course I won't fret.'

But she did. All day long the memory of Eilean's words drifted into her mind, like the shreds of a bad dream that refused to be cast away. Whenever she closed her eyes she saw Eilean's yellowy face and matted grey hair; she smelt the reek of her fishy breath, and she heard the hiss of her whisper creeping like water inside her skull:

29

She's not for you, and never will be. They'll want her back.

That night Jannet went down with Munroe to the bay. She had the baby wrapped inside a woollen shawl, wrapped again around herself, so they were bound together, mother and child. She refused to put her into a kishie basket on her back. She wanted to be able to see her all the time.

Munroe whistled a dancing tune. He had a broken tooth at the front of his mouth, making his whistle more piercing sweet than any other's. Jannet often said that she'd know it among thousands. She knew now that he was whistling with happiness at the thought of being out in his boat again. If he had heard what Eilean had said, she wondered, would he whistle so cheerfully and loud?

It was dark with no moon that night. Munroe carried a blazing peat from the fire to light their way. He lit the lantern with it to hang over the side of his boat and handed the brand back to Jannet. The other men were in the bay already, busy in the darkness, hanging their lanterns like glowing eyes. Ten men, six boats. 'We could lose them all in one go,' old Margaret had told Jannet once. 'One bad sea could take all our men away from us.'

'Go safely, Munroe,' Jannet said.

And he turned from her with a jaunty wave of his hand. The sea was in his veins, he would tell her. He was the most skilled fisherman on the island.

Behind her Jannet could hear the scraping together of notes that Eilean meant for singing. The crab-woman always followed the men down to the boats, and always sang them away. To Jannet it was a tuneless whining that made her flesh creep, especially when it came out of the shadows of the rocks. Jannet hugged her bundle to her and walked quickly past the sound. She did not want to be alone in the bay with Eilean. Yet as soon as she reached her own house she turned back.

'Am I going to spend the rest of my life fearing that woman?' she asked herself. 'How can she harm me, poor cracked soul that she is?'

Gioga was fast asleep, snug inside the shawl. Jannet held herself straight and walked steadily to Eilean's den. At least the singing had stopped. She knocked once, and pushed open the door.

4

Eilean o da Freya

Before we step inside Eilean's den we should listen
to the story she tells in her songs. The language of
her singing is strange. It has lilts and hissings in it, as
if she has listened too long to the sea. And maybe
that's true.

She came to the island as a child with the man she
called her father. He was a strange, mighty man
who was said to have rowed from the fjords of
Norway, and was remembered for his long, sleek
white hair, and for being the tallest man that any of
the islanders had ever seen. When they landed he
had heaved his boat *Freya* ashore bit by bit, until it

was high up into the shelter of rocks and away from the tide. He turned it upside down, bound it with turf and made heather ropes to lash it to the rocks. Later, he snugged it around with a wall of boulders. It became a home for them both.

They lived together in the upturned *Freya* and spoke to no one. He fished the seas for their food, and one day in a storm he was seen by other men to be washed out of his fishing boat by a massive wave. There was nothing they could do to save him. And besides, the men were superstitious. They believed that what the sea wanted to take, it would take.

The night it happened Munroe's grandmother Jaffray went down to the boat den. Somebody had to tell the girl. She found her crouching outside the boat, her hands round her knees, hiding her face. It was as if she already knew.

'Come on, Eilean. Come to me,' Grandmother Jaffray said, holding out her arms to her, trying to find a way to love the strange child. Eilean sat with her chin on her knees. Grandmother bent down to touch her, but the girl squirmed away from her, slippery as an otter. When the old woman tried to coax her up Eilean kicked and snarled until she had to let go and run for help.

'You can't stay here on your own,' the women told Eilean, shouting to make her understand. 'You'll have to come and live with one of us.'

'Don't want to,' Eilean screamed, and at last the women gave up, sorry for the child, but glad not to have her in their home. 'She's wild,' they told one another. 'Leave her.'

They took it in turns to leave food for her, and bits of clothing that their own children had grown out of. Before long she was looking after herself, catching fishes with her bare hands, setting creel pots for crabs. No other girl or woman on the island would take out a fishing boat. Eilean was not afraid of the sea.

It was Jannet's grandmother who had brought her a pony for carrying the crabs. Somebody gave her some hens. One of the men dug over the patch of grass in front of her den and planted some potatoes and cabbages. She had nothing to say to anyone in thanks, but that had been the way of her father, too.

She had a secret. Imagine her as a girl of fifteen, tall for her age. No friends, no family. Imagine her lonely ways. She liked to stand by the rocks, watching in her simple, marvelling fashion the breathing of the tide and the frill the waves made as they danced into the bay. And one night something happened that was so sharp with thrill and fright that she wondered all her life if it could have been a dream.

It began with the sound of singing. In the gleam of midnight stars she could see shapes moving in to shore. Dark heads bobbed in the sea. As they came closer to land they began to clamber up on to the rocks. Green water streamed away from them like shoals of tiny fishes. She could see the gleam of their eyes. One by one they began to stand up and move towards her, chanting in a strange, sweet, sad way, holding out their arms to her. Imagine her fear. But the spell of their singing was like a rope cast round her and hauling her towards them. She scrambled up on to her feet.

One came to her and put his arms around her. She could see the warm, dark glimmer of his eyes and the sheen of his pale hair and his skin. He lifted her up and took her to the edge of the sea, and then he dived in, and down she plunged in his arms, down and down until the darkness of the ocean grew into a bloom of light, into the billowing glow of fishes and pearls. Singing welled around her like the surge of waves. She had never known such happiness.

When she opened her eyes she was on her rock and alone. She strained to see the creatures again, but the green-black sea was still and empty. There was nothing to hear except the sighing round the rocks that the tide always made. Even so, the strange singing chimed in her head all her life. Every night she went down to the rocks to listen out for it. Sometimes in her loneliness she wished she had stayed with the strangers from the sea. She wailed out the sounds she remembered, hoping to bring them back again.

That was her secret.

And so she lived alone in a den that was kippery with smoke and littered with fish bones and crabs' backs. Seaweed dangled like crusted webs between the dim lines of drying fish; the cold sand floor gleamed. Some said she was witless, living her lonely life there, but that wasn't true. They left her alone, and shook their heads at her strange, sad wailings. She kept her secret to herself.

On the night of the storm, Eilean had heard the singing that Munroe Jaffray and Jannet had heard. She was sure the sea-people were coming back for her. She ran down to the rocks, laughing for the first time in years. When she saw Jannet there, alone and searching out the waves for Munroe, she crept into the shadows and hid. She saw Munroe bringing home the basket, and she knew what was in it. She felt something she could not even give a name to, that night. Jealousy. That's what it was.

The next day she had gone out to the skerries to see what she could find. It was more than she could wish for, that silver rag, but it was no use to her. She rowed back home and found a safe hiding place for it, in a rock pool behind her boat house. She guarded it well. One day there would be a use for it.

And now, the night after the christening, she heard Jannet come down to her boat with the child in her arms. 'Gioga,' she whispered to herself, trying out the name she had heard at the feast. She liked the sound of it. 'Gioga.'

She drew into the darkness and waited.

The reek of tar and stale fish was nearly enough to send Jannet running out for air. She thought of Munroe in his boat on the tide and wondered what he would say if he knew where she was. She lifted her bundle closer to herself. It was not an easy thing, to stand in the den that was as black as night and to know that Eilean was breathing only an arm's length away from her.

The crazed woman stood with her arms dangling at her sides and her chin jutted forwards, eyes locked into Jannet's. In the hearth the turf shifted, making both women start. A flame spurted up and lit their faces.

'I came about the bairn's gifts,' said Jannet at last. She hadn't expected to mention them.

Eilean nodded. 'Gifts from the sea.'

'And what you said. You said a strange thing.'

The baby sighed in her sleep. Eilean chuckled. She held out her hands. She was a hefty woman, with thick brown arms, which she usually kept bare. She never felt the cold as the other women did.

'You can see her,' said Jannet. Her fingers were shaking as she lifted back the shawl from Gioga's face. She squatted down on her haunches and Eilean tucked herself down, hands knuckled into her knees. Jannet could feel breath on her cheek, the fuzzle of wiry hair. 'What did you mean, Eilean?'

The crab-woman held up her right hand and splayed out her fingers and closed up her fist, and then again, and a third time.

'They'll come for her,' she said. 'Be sure of that.'

'I have never felt so cold,' said Jannet slowly. She stood up, as heavy and dull as if she was rising from the sea.

For a moment the two women stood locked. It was as if the flames of the fire stood still, and the sea on the rocks outside paused for breath. There was a right choice and a wrong choice to be made, and Jannet hovered between the two, not knowing the one from the other. Then she stepped towards Eilean, and gave her the child.

Eilean let out her breath. 'Such a wee one! Such a dab!' There was a hollow in her voice. She drew the shawl fully back and stroked the baby's face and arms, lifted up her fingers one by one and pressed her own dry cheeks to them, breathed in Gioga's hair, and all the time rocking, rocking from side to side, and going *wheesh! wheesh!* in her mouth, stooping to catch the light of the fire in Gioga's eyes, *wheesh! wheesh!* till Jannet could bear it no longer. She snatched back the baby and ran for home, her face pressed into the shawls. When she was safe in the light of her own fire she unwrapped the baby and looked down at her. Gioga gazed back, her dark eyes not moving or blinking.

'I'll never let you go,' Jannet whispered. 'They'll not have you, whoever they are.'

5

Hill Marliner

Gioga was a child of twelve months when the stranger came for her. She had begun to take her first tottering steps, and could speak the words 'Mam' and 'Da' and a few others to make her needs understood. She was loved by everyone, especially the children from the other crofts. Harris adored her. He lived with Morag and his father and brothers right up beyond Round Hill, a mile or more from Jannet's cottage, but he came down every day to see the baby. He loved to coax her to walk, and it was when she was holding his hand that she made her first swaying attempts to stand up. He would half carry her, half lead her gently and patiently down to the bay, bring her shells to play with, and sit with her while she poured sand between her fingers.

Sometimes Eilean would come and squat by them. Like all the children, Harris was afraid of her, but it was quite clear that Gioga was not. The woman would sit near to them and sing her odd songs, and Gioga, tiny as she was, began to pick up the fragments of tune and hum them, thoughtlessly. When she heard her Jannet would frown and try to teach her nursery songs.

And when Eilean came, she would tell stories about the sea. Sometimes they would be wonderful, magical tales, and sometimes they would be so frightening that they would leave Harris fretful at night.

'Did I tell you about the lord of the oceans?' Eilean said to them one day, and Harris shook his head, not looking at her but punching his fists into the sand to show that he had been told not to listen to her stories. Gioga gazed at the crab-woman.

'The lord of the oceans rides the waves from morning till night, from ice to ice, from the world's end to the world's end,' said Eilean in her crooning way. 'He wears a billowing cloak that has all the colours of the sea in it, grey at times, or blue or brown. Green with the dawn, or crimson with the setting sun. His long white hair streams out behind him.'

'Have you ever seen him?' asked Harris, gazing in spite of himself at the green billowing waves with their white manes.

'Aye. I've seen him. Many a time. I've heard him, too.'

'He's not there today, is he?' Harris asked, suddenly anxious.

Eilean stood up and moved away from them. She stood with her arms folded, staring out to the horizon. 'He may be. He may come here today.'

'What for?'

'To find what is his. Even though he may lose his life for it.'

Harris needed to think about this. He pretended he hadn't heard her. He carried on with the castle he was making out of sand. Gioga clamped shells on to the turrets, laughingly squashing her fist down whenever Harris warned her to be gentle.

'What is it he looks for?' he asked, pretending he was talking to himself.

'His own,' said Eilean, 'that is lost.' She seemed to have forgotten about the children.

'What we need is a banner to fly on the castle,' said Harris, glancing round.

'Banner,' agreed Gioga.

'A feather will do it!' Harris ran off to where he could see a gull's white feather just slanting from sand, like a fallen arrow. As he ran towards it the feather lifted up in a sudden surge of breeze, and Harris hurled himself after it, shouting with laughter. Gioga pulled herself unsteadily on to her feet and began to totter after him, then stopped.

She thought she could hear Filean singing, but it seemed to come from the sea. She dropped on to her knees and crawled to the creamy edge of the water. The tide was coming in quickly now. The song came again, low like the wind. She crawled on, into the icy-cold water. It splashed against her arms and into her face. She closed her eyes and held up her head, spluttering as the salty waves winded her. She tried to stand up, pushing herself against the rocking of the tide, fell backwards, came up coughing and still pushed forward. The song drifted towards her like flotsam just out of reach. Again she fell and the waves surged over her.

'Gioga! Bad girl! Bad!' She was suddenly scooped up by Harris. He held her tightly in his arms and plunged back towards the sand with her. 'Mustn't do that!' he told her.

She wriggled in his grasp, trying to kick herself free as he struggled to run with her. She twisted her head round and held out her arms towards the sea.

'It's all right,' he whispered, trying to soothe her. He was nearly sobbing with fright. 'Don't wail. You're safe now.'

Up by the rock steps Eilean was standing and watching, her arms folded under her shawl, her head to one side.

'Did you not see her fall in?' Harris shouted. 'Why didn't you save her?'

'She did not fall in,' said Eilean. 'And she was safe enough with the sea.'

Harris pushed past her, frightened by the strange knowing smile on her face. He ran stumbling to the croft house with Gioga tight in his arms.

'What happened?' asked Jannet, as the two crying children burst in.

'She fell in the sea.' Harris was sobbing properly now. He was more frightened of Eilean's strangeness than of anything else.

'And you rescued her.' Jannet took the baby from him and rocked her gently, trying to soothe them both. She changed Gioga into dry clothes and warmed a drink for them over the fire. The baby soon drifted into her afternoon sleep. Harris sat by her cradle, peering anxiously down at her until he was quite sure that she was sleeping peacefully.

'I'll go back up now to Mam,' he said.

'You do,' Jannet told him. 'And don't fret any more. The wee one's fine, see.'

But still Harris lingered, his finger tracing the little figures of fishes and stars Munroe had carved along the cradle's rim. He had things to tell Jannet about that morning, but he couldn't put his thoughts into words. At last he went, with fear still bruising him.

Jannet had almost forgotten the incident. Feeling drowsy herself, she sat in the sunlight that streamed through the door, listening to Gioga's quiet sighing. The tide was nearly at its height, and the constant surge and hiss of spray was like a lullaby to her. Soon Munroe would be home and she would go down to prepare the fish he had caught, but here in the sunshine with the tide singing to her she drifted away into dreams.

A sudden hammering made her jump to her feet. A tall man stood in the doorway. He was draped in a full grey cloak that fell to his feet, and his hair was long and white. She had never seen him before, or anyone like him, and she was deeply afraid.

He came into the room and stood looking down at the cradle where Gioga lay sleeping.

'If it's Munroe you're after, he's out on the sea,' Jannet whispered.

'I know well where he is,' said the stranger. 'But it's not him I'm seeking. I've come for my child.'

Munroe Jaffray was way out to sea, getting ready to turn before the tide changed. The fishing had not been good, but the day was fine and clear. Sunlight sparkled like stars on the water, and the heat reflected up on to his face. A solitary gull cruised across the sky. At that very moment when the stranger spoke to Jannet, Munroe's skin went cold. He stood up to reach for his jacket and as he did so his boat began to rock wildly. He tumbled forward, caught the side of the boat to save himself, and saw that the sea around him was teeming with fishes, flashing and leaping, streaming like silver ribbons. He could hardly believe what he saw. He cast his net over the side and hauled in his catch, and again and again. At last, exhausted, he slumped back and began to row for home. There was a month's store caught in one day.

★

'You've made a mistake. This is my child,' said Jannet to the stranger. She lifted Gioga out of her cradle, holding her tightly. She needed her sleepy warmth. She was cold with fright herself.

'No. You are her nurse. But you've treated her well,' the man said. 'And I owe you a fee for that.'

'You don't owe me anything. I won't take anything from you.' Jannet could hardly speak for the fear in her throat.

'I have paid your husband well.' The man held out his hands. She couldn't see his face for the darkness of the room. 'Let me take her now.'

'She knows me as her mother. She loves me.'

'I can see that.'

'And how do I know you're her father? Who are you? Where do you come from?' She knew she was gabbling out her questions. In her frenzied mind was the thought that Munroe must come home soon, and that when the stranger saw them together he would know how good they were as parents. She had no doubt that he spoke the truth. Hadn't Gioga been found alone in the rock pool? Somebody had put her there. Hadn't Eilean warned her that she wouldn't be able to keep her?

'My name is Hill Marliner,' the man said. 'I travel

47

far and wide in the oceans. Let me see her, good nurse.'

Jannet sank down on to her stool and sat Gioga upright on her knee. The child was beginning to wake up, rubbing her fists into her eyes and yawning. Hill Marliner leaned forward, murmuring something in a strange tongue, and the child turned her head to look at him. She stared at him thoughtfully, almost dreamily. He reached out his hand and Jannet clenched her arms round Gioga, but all he did was to stroke the child's hair and her cheek. His eyes were bright and his movements were soft and gentle.

It seemed as if that moment lasted for ever, while outside herring gulls screamed to welcome in the fishing boats, their voices loud and shrill and laughing. At last Hill Marliner stood up.

'She is happy,' he said. 'She may stay with you a little longer. But I will come back.'

As soon as he had gone Jannet put the protesting Gioga down in her cot, ran outside and closed the door firmly behind her. There was no sign of the man.

She ran over the grass to the houses at the top of the hill.

'Have you seen a stranger come by?' she shouted

48

to Grandfather Jaffray as he hobbled out of his doorway to throw grain to his hens.

'There's been no one come by all day,' he told her.

Fearing again, Jannet ran back, picked up her child and took her down to the bay. There was Eilean, standing arms folded and watching the sea.

Jannet saw that the men were home. She began to feel calm again. She knew she couldn't tell Munroe about Hill Marliner. In his honest, simple way Munroe would feel he must give back Gioga, might even set up a search for the man who claimed to be her father. Jannet felt frantic at the thought of parting with Gioga now. It was better not to tell.

'Jannet, come down!' Munroe shouted, seeing her there. 'I've never had my boat so full of fish!'

The other men had come to his boat to wonder at his haul. It had been a poor day for them.

No. She would not spoil his joy with dark news. She steadied Gioga on the shingle and walked her down to the boat, and Munroe lifted the laughing child up to see the fishes he had caught.

'You've a grand harvest there, Munroe Jaffray,' said Eilean, coming to stand by them. 'You'll be needing all the help you can get.'

'We'll manage fine,' said Jannet, cold and polite.

'Can I mind the bairn out of your way, perhaps, while you get on?'

It was a decent offer, and Munroe began to thank her.

'No,' said Jannet. 'We'll manage.'

All the same, when Eilean walked away to her boat house Jannet gazed after her for a long, quiet time. It was as if they shared a secret, the two women, and would be bonded by it for ever.

6

The Second Visit

Seven years later the stranger came back. Jannet had long stopped watching out for him. The heather was growing pale on the cliffs, and late summer hazes were low on the land. The wind soughed over fields of corn ripe for harvesting. The sea was warm that day.

'Could I come out on the boat with you, Da?' Gioga asked on that morning. 'And can Harris come too?'

'Harris has plenty to do, now he's the beach boy. He has to salt the fish for winter,' said Munroe.

'I don't want her to go on the sea,' said Jannet.

'The sea is for men to work on,' Munroe agreed.

'I don't want her to go,' Jannet repeated.

Gioga followed Munroe down to the rocks, and stood by him when he was piling the nets into his boat.

'What's my princess up to now?' he asked, smiling down at her.

'Just take me out to the skerries,' she pleaded. 'Then you can bring me back and go out fishing on your own.'

'The skerries?' Munroe narrowed his eyes. He well remembered the night of the singing sea and the pale bundle caught between the rocks. He had never taken his boat there since. 'What's so special about the skerries?'

'They look like monsters in the sea.'

'Aye, they do that,' Munroe laughed. 'With scaly backs and foam spitting out of their mouths. You'd not want to go out there.'

'Not that far then. Just out of the bay a little, and then home again. I want to come, Da.'

She had a way of winning Munroe round. He lifted her into the boat and pushed out, then jumped in after her and hauled up the sail. As the boat slid along the smooth water Gioga leaned back and trailed her hand over the edge. She could see Harris working with his father and brothers, setting up the salmon nets. Away on the shore she could hear the sweet piping of the oyster-catchers. She could see the hunched stone croft house with its thatched roof, its lazy drift of blue smoke. Jannet would be making jams for the winter store. And on the cliffs where the gannets screamed, she could see Eilean o da Freya.

From far out at sea came a long wailing cry, and another, and more. It was then Gioga knew why she had wanted to come out with Munroe that day, and she knew what she wanted to do. She daren't look at him, in case he read it in her eyes and tried to stop her. She must bide her time. A skein of geese flew out from land, low, with their necks outstretched and their wingbeats shimmying the air. As Munroe looked up at them she took her moment, stood up slowly, and dived from the side of the boat.

'No!' she heard Munroe shout. He was afraid for her, but he should not have been. Like many fishermen he could not swim himself. The sea was not for playing in. He knew that Gioga had never been in the sea before, except to splash and jump with Harris when the tide was coming in.

She was not afraid. The water was silky soft against her skin, as smooth as air. She rolled down into its bluey-greenness, spiralling slowly round to see the sunlight filtering through like gold. Birds like fishes swam on the other side of the water, fishes drifted up to her like leaves. Dark shapes loomed and flicked away again, greeny-black in the strange light. She could hear the clear, sweet wailing all around her; and from what seemed like a million miles away, Munroe's voice, calling her back. She did not want to go to him.

As she swam up to the surface she could see his hands stretched out to her. His face was puckering with frowns as he leaned over to haul her back into the boat. She laughed up at him and he held her close, wet through though she was.

'My little fish, did you fall in?' he murmured. 'See, you're safe now, you're quite safe.'

But she pulled away from him and leaned over the side as if she was longing to be back in the water again. Munroe knew then that it had been no accident, that she hadn't fallen in by chance. He saw in the brightness of her eyes and the wistful tilt of her head that she longed to be back in the water, and he was fearful. He would not tell Jannet about it. He rowed straight to the bay and called to Harris to run up to the house with Gioga and to stay with her if Jannet wasn't at home.

'Have you drowned yourself?' Harris asked her, teasing.

'No,' she said. 'I can swim all right.'

'I can't.' Harris shivered. 'And I don't want to.' He was superstitious about the water, like his father and uncle. 'What did you see down there? Ghosts of drowned men? They float down there for ever, if they don't turn into gulls in time.'

She looked at him, surprised. 'I didn't see them. I saw castles and fields right under the sea. Next time I want to swim right down.'

'Don't let your da hear you say that,' Harris crowed, 'or he'll never let you on his boat again.'

He delivered her to Jannet, who scolded her and told her to sit by the fire to dry her clothes. Harris was sent back to his netting with a crust of new bread in his hand. And in the steamy house where jam was bubbling and frothing in its cauldron over the fire and new bread was cooling on stones, Gioga dreamed of the sea. She looked into the fire and saw waves and fronds of weeds. In the purring of the flames she heard the flickering of fishes. The sight and sound of the sea would never go out of her mind again, but would lie like the lapping tide itself, as true a part of her as the blood flowing in her veins.

'You could help me now,' said Jannet, breaking into her reverie. 'Wipe the warm pots round and hold them steady while I pour in the jam.' The jam was boiling deeply in its cauldron, and as Gioga peered in to watch the softened fruit bulging in its liquid she did not hear the stranger come in. What she did hear was Jannet's quick gasp, and she looked round to see her standing with her hand to her mouth, and behind her Hill Marliner in his cloak of oceans.

'Go up to your aunt's,' Jannet said, her voice tight and cold and a strange thing to hear. But Gioga couldn't move. The man stared at her, and she stared up at the man. Odd and striking though he was, and unlike anybody she had ever seen before, she felt drawn to him. It was almost as if she knew him. Steam from the pot and smoke from the fire curled around him. It was hard to see his face in the dark room with the sunlight behind him.

'Didn't I tell you I would come back?' said Hill Marliner to Jannet.

'You did.' She could hardly speak for the bursting of her heart. She grasped out for Gioga and pushed her towards the light of the door. 'Go, Gioga,' she said. 'Go.'

And the child, frightened by the voice she was hearing, did as she was told at last, and ran.

But she never reached Morag's house. Eilean stopped her on her way.

'Where are you off to with the wind at your heels?' she asked.

'Mam sent me to my Aunt Morag's.'

'And I saw Morag setting off just this minute, to fetch driftwood,' said Eilean.

Gioga stopped, uncertain what to do. She wanted to see the stranger again, but she daren't go back to the house till Jannet sent for her. 'Maybe I'll wait just here,' she said. 'Till Mam comes for me.'

'Come over here,' said Eilean, 'and watch the selkies over by the skerry rocks.' And she took the child's hand and led her to the very edge of the cliffs.

'It will do you no good to hide her,' said Hill Marliner to Jannet.

She stood with her arms folded and her back against the door. Dread was surging through her like the slow beat of a drum, like the steady pummelling of waves against rocks. It would never go away, till the end of her life. She would always remember that day when she stood between Hill Marliner and her child. Munroe was out at sea. Gioga's discarded wooden doll lay on the floor. She must keep the stranger there until Gioga had reached Morag's. That was the least she could do to try to save the child.

'If she really is your child, why did you leave her in the skerry rocks to drown?' she demanded.

'She would not have drowned. She was a gift,' said Hill Marliner.

'Then if she was a gift, why take her back?'

'She was not your gift. She was meant for another.'

Jannet couldn't bear to look at him. She thought of Eilean, alone and prowling the bay night after night, trailing her crabbing pony over the sands, staring out from the cliff tops. She tried to push the woman out of her mind, but Eilean clung on like a limpet to a rock.

'And the other would know that she could not keep her. That I would return for my child one day.'

'I know too,' said Jannet quietly. 'But not yet. Please, not yet.'

'I have paid you well for your kindness to her, but here's more.'

Hill Marliner's cloak of oceans sighed as he drew from it a skin purse and placed it in Jannet's hands. She let it drop to the floor. Gold coins rolled out.

She walked past him and ran up the long hill to the far croft, where Morag lived.

Her sister was washing clothes in the burn behind her house. When she saw Jannet's face she dropped her bundle of washing and ran to her.

'Whatever has happened?' she asked.

Jannet shook her head, unable to tell anything of the truth. 'Where's Gioga? I have to take her home.'

But Morag only frowned with puzzlement. 'I've been here all morning,' she said. 'I've not seen her, Jannet.'

Though fear leapt like a fish in Jannet's heart, Gioga was quite safe. She was sitting with Eilean on the cliff top, looking down to the far rocks of the skerries.

'That's where the selkies lie,' said Eilean to the child. 'The people who live in the sea.'

'They're seals, not people. They're like the fish.' Gioga was staring out to the far rocks, searching for what she might see out there.

'They live everywhere in the oceans,' Eilean told her. 'But they're not fishes. At sea they long for the land, and on the land they long for the sea. They haunt and trouble the men who make them live in the sea.'

Below them seagulls squabbled on their cliff perches. Two white fulmars lifted themselves away and floated stiff-winged down to the water.

'It was on account of those birds that the seals began,' said Eilean. 'Did I tell you the story of the girl who was loved by a fulmar?'

'No.' Gioga did not think she wanted to hear it.

'Loved by a fulmar, and frightened by it,' Eilean went on in her crooning way. 'And one day the girl's father decided to take her away from the fulmar, to hide her from it. He rowed her out to sea and the fulmar followed croaking and spitting, and wheeling after them like those fulmars down there. It landed on the boat, tore at the man, tore at his skin and his hair in its passion to have the girl. The man was so frightened by the bird that he tried to kill it, but he hadn't the strength to do it. So what do you think he did?'

'I don't know,' whispered Gioga.

'He threw his daughter over the side of the boat. He thought that the fulmar would leave him then. But the girl clung on to the boat, tried to climb back in, with the fulmar screaming and beating its wings around her. And her father, with fear in his heart, cut off her fingers to make her let go.'

Gioga put her hands over her face.

'Those fingers turned into the seals of the ocean,' said Eilean. 'Those selkies you see today have come down from the daughter who gave up her life. That's why they moan and cry around the rocks. That's why they come into shore and stare at the people on land. That's why they know us so well.'

'I've heard them crying in the night,' said Gioga.

'There's an old bull seal that I like to look out for,' said Eilean to the child. 'He's a mighty one, with his white head and his deep voice. Limpets and periwinkles grow in his cheeks, he's so old. He's the king of the seals. The first time I cast eyes on him, would you know who I thought he was?' She looked down at the girl, who shook her head solemnly.

'My father,' said Eilean softly. 'That's who he reminded me of. My old father, who never came back from the sea.'

7

The Haven

There is no telling the relief that Jannet felt when she returned to her house to find Gioga safe inside. But the child had changed in that time, and Jannet had too. There was a dreaminess about Gioga, in her eyes and in her voice, in the way she listened to a sound inside her head. And Jannet had grown hard and jealous, wanting to know what Eilean had told Gioga. When Munroe came home she smothered the memory of Hill Marliner's visit, just as she had smothered his gold coins with ash from the fire. Munroe found himself to be apart from her, and did not know how to touch her again. During the night

Jannet lay wide-eyed beside him, listening out in the darkness.

'What is it?' Munroe asked.

'Nothing,' she told him. 'Sleep.'

And soon the sound she had been listening out for came – a padding of feet on the stones. Jannet sat up sharp, pulled her gown round her and walked over the cold floor to the far end of the room. There in the moonlight was Gioga, about to leave the house and run out into the night. Her hair was loose and wild around her face, and her eyes were like still water, with no life in them.

Jannet took the child's hand and led her back to her sleeping place. She sat by her until grey dawn came. And in all this time, Gioga did not wake up; nor did she sleep.

'Gioga is not well,' said Jannet the next morning.

Gioga and Munroe stared at each other.

'She is pale,' Munroe agreed. 'The sea may have chilled her yesterday when she fell in.'

'It's more than a chill. I think I should take her over the water to see the healer.'

Munroe shrugged. 'Morag will have a cure for her. She always has something.'

'I don't want a cure,' said Gioga. 'I want to see Eilean.'

'You will not.' Jannet took the girl firmly by the hand. 'You'll stay with me today. We'll go over the moors to Reeversend. There's some fine seaweed now, for the fields. I'll need your help.'

Up on the moors the wind was bleak and wild. The ponies were running free, their manes and tails streaming. Gioga and Harris raced to catch them and led them to where women were raking up juicy piles of seaweed down in the bay. All day Gioga and the other children scrambled up and down the skiddy rock steps, loading up the ponies' baskets. At the end of the line Eilean worked alone. Gioga kept glancing across to her, but knew by the tightening of Jannet's mouth that she mustn't go near the crab-woman. She wanted more tales of the selkies that lived out on the skerries and under the ocean, that watched her from the bay. Whenever she closed her eyes she pictured the greeny-gold of the water and the dark shapes looming towards her.

By the end of the afternoon Jannet and Morag were the last on the beach. Already the light in the sky was growing dim.

'Can I go with Harris this time?' Gioga asked.

Jannet stood with her arms akimbo, nursing her aching back.

'All right,' she said. 'You've worked well. But stay with him.'

Gioga ran after Harris, whistling like him as he urged the loaded ponies over the moors. He had already been to Gioga's croft that day, emptying out the baskets on to the fields, spreading the seaweed to feed the soil. When they reached his own croft he tipped the baskets next to the stacks of drying peat. 'Tomorrow will do for the spreading,' he said. Gioga threw down some carrots for the little ponies. She was lost in thought all the time she worked.

'Are you awake?' Harris asked. She said nothing.

'I have a puzzle for you,' he said. 'I stand on one leg with my heart in my head. What am I?'

But Gioga was not listening. 'Harris? Do you know of the selkies?'

He wiped his brow with the back of his hand. In spite of the cold wind the working was hot.

'Of course I know of the selkies,' he said.

'But do you know where they came from?' She told him Eilean's story about the fulmar.

'That's an awful scary tale,' he said. 'If it's true.' He slapped the ponies to send them away, and stood watching as they galloped back over the hill to their moors, hooves thudding, manes flowing.

'I want to go right out to the skerries to see them close.'

'We don't have to go out to the skerries,' he said. 'They're with their pups right now, in some of the bays. We can see them from the Klingrie hole. But you didn't guess my riddle.'

He vaulted a low wall protecting the long-stalked cabbages and heaved one out of the earth.

'I knew all the time,' Gioga said, 'and you'd better stick that one back in before your mother beats you with it.'

Not far from Morag's croft there was a huge hole in the ground, near the edge of the cliff. Harris's father had told him it had been made long ago when the roof of a cave had fallen in. The walls of the cavern were steep and high, and at the bottom the sea churned in through a little cave mouth. It was so dangerous that both the children had been forbidden ever to go near it, in case they fell over the edge. 'If you don't break your neck by falling down there, the sea will pull you out and drown you,' Jannet had warned them.

As they drew near the Klingrie hole, Harris dropped down on to his hands and knees and crawled to the very edge, then flattened himself and stretched out on his belly.

'They're here,' he called.

Gioga stretched herself out beside him and looked down into the sheltered cavern that lay far below them. They could hear the drumming of the tide around it. But there in the quiet coves and rock shelves that the tide didn't reach, seal mothers lay suckling their pups.

'Just look at them!' breathed Gioga. 'It tingles my spine to see them like that.'

'They're fine enough when they're in the water. They poke their heads up like dogs, and look at you straight.' Harris laughed. 'But when you see them on land, they're just like fat slugs. I don't like them.'

'I wish I could see them closer,' said Gioga. 'The pups.'

'I could show you the place where they sleep.'

'Can you?'

'I'll show you tonight if you dare to come in the dark. When the tide's full up, I'll show you then.'

Darkness soon comes in the land of the north at the end of the year. The sun was down by the time the day's work was done. The sky was as dim as the sea. Raggedy crows croaked from the fence posts as the crofters made their way home.

'Can we see them now?' said Gioga.

'No, not yet,' said Harris. 'The tide isn't high

enough. We have to get right to the selkie hole.'

'But if I go home now Mam won't let me out again.'

'Can Gioga eat with us tonight?' Harris called out to Jannet, just as she was ready to turn down towards her croft.

'Yes, if you bring her back home.'

When they reached his house Harris and Gioga ate oat cakes and herring, and watched for the darkness to settle. It didn't take long. They could hear the sea streaming into the shore, and when Harris's father came home, bone weary and raw with the cold, they knew that the tide was in.

'Is it time now?' Gioga whispered.

Harris nodded to her. He lit a brand in the fire and they went down to the bay together to where the boats were beached.

They pushed the smallest boat down to the water and climbed in. Harris took up the oars and Gioga held up the slow-burning brand. There was no moon or stars, only the blackness of sky and sea all around them, like the dark before dreams. And there was no sound on the sea that night but the dip and swish of the oars, and the lapping of water against the creaking boat. Neither Harris nor Gioga spoke.

One by one the stars began to glimmer through, though their light was hardly sure enough to soften the darkness.

At last Harris guided the little boat up against the cliff and pulled in the oars.

'They'll be in there,' he said, 'in that hole.'

Gioga held up the brand and could just make out in front of her a dark cave mouth cut into the rock.

'I went in there once with my da,' Harris told her. 'That's where the seals have their nursery.'

'Can we go in?' Gioga asked.

'No,' Harris whispered. 'I daren't go back in. They'll come snarling at us if we go near them. But that's where they'll be.'

Gioga said nothing then. She could hear low voices from inside the cave, and the mewling of babies. She stuck her brand in the rowlock where the oar had rested and slipped over the side of the boat into the water.

'Are you going in there? You'll freeze.' Harris's voice was a cormorant's croak in the darkness. 'You'll need the light.'

Gioga reached up and lifted the brand out of the rowlock, and swam with it, holding it just in front of her, so its light bobbed like a tiny moon on the water. And into the hole she went.

The light of her torch licked across the walls of the cave and over its glistening rocks, pink and green and sparking silver. Low waves slapped against them. Shadow and flame-light danced together. Gioga trod water and gazed around her.

There were still, quiet shapes in the darkness, there were eyes turned towards her. There was a breathlessness and a waiting, and a watching all around her. She swam forward slowly and one of the seals slid into the water and swam alongside her, face turned towards her all the time, eyes fixed on Gioga's. They were twin shadows on the flickering water, Gioga and the she-seal, gliding and turning as one.

'Gioga, are you all right in there?' came Harris's voice, shrill with fear, and instantly the seal shadow sank, and the dark shapes on the rocks slithered into the water, pups on their mother's backs. There was a mewing, like the crying of a lamb, and a sad, low moaning, and then all was silent again.

Gioga kicked on to her back and swam out of the cave mouth and up to the boat. Harris hauled her in and then rowed home. They were both shaking by now.

'You're wet to the skin,' he said, 'and Jannet will be raging at me for not taking care of you.'

He muttered and grumbled all the way home, but Gioga was not listening to him. She had done what she wanted to do. She had seen what she wanted to see: the seal pups in their silky white coats. She had heard their voices, and she could hear them still in her head. What Harris was saying made no sense to her at all. She couldn't listen to him. In silence they dragged the boat on to the shingle. Rabbits scuttled away from them as they ran barefoot over the dunes.

'I'll leave you here,' said Harris, dithering on the hilltop. Only two houses showed their lanterns, his and Gioga's, far apart in the peat-dark night. He knew he should take Gioga to her own house, but he was afraid of what Jannet might say to him.

'I don't mind,' and Gioga slipped like a mouse out of the light of his brand before he had a chance to repent.

'Where have you been?' Jannet demanded, when Gioga ran in on her own into the house and stood dripping in front of the hearth.

'I swam with the selkies,' Gioga laughed.

'Dry yourself and go to bed.' It was all Jannet said to her, but Gioga had seen the sudden rush of anger and distress on Jannet's face, and heard a coldness in her voice that she did not recognize. What she did not see, as she turned away from the heaped ash of the hearth, was how Jannet stood swaying with her knuckles pressed to her mouth and her eyes closed. Gioga went down to the far end of the room and crept between the cows for warmth. Their slow breathing comforted her, and before long she drifted into a sleep where seals buoyed her along a gently rocking sea.

Next morning she ran straight to Eilean's den.

'I've seen the seals,' she shouted, breathless with excitement. 'I went to their cave.'

'Ah, the selkies,' said Eilean.

'They make a strange sound. I always thought it was the seagulls I could hear.'

Eilean laughed. 'They don't sound like gulls.'

'No,' said Gioga. 'They sound like people. They have the voices of men and women. The young ones cry like babies.'

'What did you see?'

Gioga tried to recall the dark shapes, and the gleaming watchful eyes she had seen in her torch-light the night before.

'I saw a baby, as white as a lamb. And I swam with a seal.'

'You were not afraid of them.'

'No. Harris was afraid to go in with me, but I wasn't afraid of them. I wanted to stay with them.'

'I know that,' said Eilean.

'But then Harris called out to me, and they all slithered into the water and disappeared. I felt frightened then. I felt lonely in the big dark cave.'

'They like the company of people,' Eilean told her. 'People like their company. Even so men kill them for their skins. But the seal-killers will always be troubled for what they've done.'

Harris had seen Gioga with Eilean and came running across the rocks towards them. He sat down with them, leaning against the side of Eilean's boat. She was stringing fish for the winter, hanging them up on lines to dry across her room, to be slowly smoked by her fire. At home Harris's mother was doing the same thing.

'I know of the seal-killers,' said Harris, picking up her last words. 'My grandfather was one.'

'Then you'll know the story of the man who was asked to kill a hundred seals,' said Eilean.

'I think I do,' said Harris.

'But I don't,' Gioga said. 'Da and Mam don't talk about the seals, ever.'

'Then I'll tell you,' said Eilean. 'This man killed a seal one day for oil for his lamps, and skin for his clothes and his shoes. And at the end of the day a stranger came into his house and asked about the seals he'd killed. "I killed one and one escaped. I think it was wounded," the seal-killer said. "My master has sent me to ask you to kill a hundred seals," said the stranger, "and here's money for it." He threw him a purse full of gold. "That's a great many seals," said the seal-killer. "Will you come to speak to my master about it?" asked the stranger. The seal-killer agreed, and the stranger took him outside and mounted the man up on his white horse behind him and they rode off into the night.'

'I do know this story,' interrupted Harris. 'I remember the white horse.' He was stilled by Gioga's glance.

'They rode on into the night,' Eilean went on, 'until they came to the very edge of a cliff, where they dismounted. "And where is your master?" asked the seal-killer. The stranger put his arms round him and blew into his mouth, and leapt with him over the cliff and down and down with him into the sea. And there they saw houses made of pearl and coral, of all the colours you can imagine. "I have tricked you," said the stranger, "but I want you to meet my father." There, on a rock bed, lay an old man, dying. "I am the seal you wounded today," said the old man. "My only cure is if you will heal my wounds with your hands. Only your hands can do it." The seal-killer was bitterly sad to see the wounds he had made in the old man. He put his hands on him and the wounds were healed. And then the old man said, "You must promise never to kill seals again, but leave them to live in the sea. If you do not promise you will never return to land." When he'd promised that, the stranger put his arms around him again, and they swam up and up, and arrived back at the cliff. There the stranger blew into his mouth and the man returned to his home.'

'And did he keep his promise?' asked Gioga.

'There were no more seals killed by that man or his family.' Eilean looked at Harris. 'That's true, isn't it?'

The boy nodded.

'Now that you know the selkies,' Eilean said to Gioga, 'you will never sleep because the tide will be always flowing through you. You'll be listening and watching always for its comings and goings.'

The skerries loomed in the sea-mist. Hidden gulls cried out and from far off came the bleak lament of a seal.

Harris was wanting to go. He could see Jannet

coming towards them, driving her sheep down to the shore to feed on the seaweed there. He pulled Gioga's arm.

'I wish I could understand what it is they say to each other,' Gioga said.

'One day you'll find that out too,' Eilean promised. 'But not yet.'

'Do you know their language?' Gioga asked. She was unwilling to move.

Harris laughed sharply. He stood up with his hands in his pockets, distancing himself from the girl and the woman, in case Jannet blamed him for finding them together.

'There is a way of understanding the selkies,' said Eilean. 'And one day I'll teach it to you.' She gathered up her strings of fish and went back into her boat house before Jannet reached them.

Jannet was wearing her walking shoes and carrying a full kishie on her back. She came up to the two children and stood looking down at Gioga.

'Come with me quickly,' she said to Gioga. 'We're catching the market ferry to the mainland.'

There was no rush about her, no need to suspect what she had in her mind. Gioga had never been on the ferry, and the thought of a journey excited her.

Harris ran down with them to the little harbour where the ferry boat came over from Mainland.

Eilean followed them down and stood watching. 'This will do you no good,' she said, as Jannet hurried past her.

But if Jannet heard, she said nothing. She bundled Gioga over the rocks that were slippery with weed. The sea-mist hung like a quiet breath around them. Gioga waved goodbye to Harris. 'I'll bring you something back,' she promised. 'What would you like?'

Harris stood with his feet apart and his left arm crooked out in front of him. His right arm swung to and fro across his body.

'And I'll dance to your fiddle,' she laughed, 'tomorrow.'

She clambered in after Jannet and sat with her among the lobster creels and crates of salted fish, the tethered geese and lambs. The ferryman rowed away from the island, past the ghostly rocks and the skerries, out and away into the mist. Eilean was a speck left alone on the shore, and all around in the sea came the dark bobbing heads of the seals.

8

The Valley of Silence

'Will we get back tonight?' Gioga wanted to know.

'No, not tonight.'

That was all right. Jannet often stayed over on Mainland if she went to market, especially if the seas were too rough for the ferry.

'But where will we stay?'

'With my cousin, if she'll have us.'

'Where does she live?'

They had landed on the other side of the water. Gioga stared round at the deserted jetty. Apart from a few ponies and handcarts which were waiting to be piled up with fish there was no sign of anybody living there.

'I'm not sure,' Jannet told her. 'I've heard from her only once since she moved away from the island. I've never been to see her place. But I know it's a good walk from here.'

Gioga couldn't understand why Jannet was so anxious and distracted. There seemed to be no excitement for her in the journey.

'Why are we going to see her?'

'Because we have to, Gioga. I'm going to ask her to look after you for a bit.'

She had set off at a brisk pace along the muddy track, and Gioga had to run to keep up with her.

'But I don't want to stay here, not without you. And what about Da?'

Jannet would answer none of her questions.

'How long will I have to stay here? Will it be more than two days?'

Still Jannet didn't answer. The boggy track took them over brown hills and snaking peaty burns. Gioga kept turning round, anxious in case they lost sight of the sea, but Jannet urged her on.

'Hurry, Gioga. We must get there before dark or we'll be sleeping out on the grass.'

When the light was drained from the sky they

arrived at a small croft. 'Is this it?' asked Gioga.

'I don't think so.' Jannet knocked at the door of the house and was welcomed in by the old woman who lived there. She gave them soup and bread in exchange for the dried fish Jannet offered her from her bundle. As they ate she sat watching them, nodding and sighing, almost asleep by the fire. Cards of wool lay around her feet. A hen chuttered to itself on a beam, a comfortable sound that made Gioga yearn for home. The old woman's husband came in with a rabbiting gun over his shoulder and, for a moment, drowsy by the fire, Gioga thought it might be Munroe come to fetch them back.

'I'm wanting to find my cousin Madelaine,' Jannet told the couple. 'She's married to a man named Rab, but I don't know his other name. He breeds ponies and sells them at local fairs.'

The old woman nodded. 'I know him,' she said. Her face was whiskery and her hair wisped like a white cloud around the rim of her bonnet. As she sat she pulled wool from a shank at her feet and wound it around her fingers. Her cats tugged idly at the wool as it snaked past them.

'And can you tell me where they live?'

'They live a good way from here, too far for you to walk tonight.'

'I know it's far,' Jannet said. 'I know it's a long way from the sea. Madelaine told me that.'

'Oh yes, it is that,' the old woman agreed. 'About as far from the sea as you can get.'

'We seem to have come a long way already,' said Jannet. 'We've left the sea a good way behind us.'

'I can still hear it,' said Gioga, her eyes wide with listening. 'It's getting very soft but I can hear it.'

Jannet looked at her and nodded. 'I thought so. We'd better get you to my cousin's as soon as possible.'

'That child needs her sleep,' said the old woman. 'Spend the night here, by the fire. And tomorrow you can set off early on your way. My man can take you there. Too far for my old legs!'

Gioga didn't sleep that night, although she was tired from walking. She sat by the window and strained to hear the sea. She could hear the moan of the wind outside the house, the click of needles and the murmur of voices as the two women knitted and gossiped by the fire. But she was listening through their sounds to the distant whispering of the tide. She was alert to all its movements around the bays of her island, and to the voices beneath the surface, on the bed of the sea.

★

There is no describing how the track meandered through valleys and between lochans the next day. The old man plodded slowly on, and Gioga and Jannet were obliged to walk at his pace. At last they came to a steep hill that was too stony for him to climb. 'Over the top,' he wheezed. 'Nothing else there but Rab's croft, so you'll see it fine. I'll wait for you here,' he told Jannet.

Up and away from him they climbed, and walked along the ridge and into a valley that was so steep-sided and gloomy that it seemed as if the sun had forsaken it. It was wrapped in a deep silence, as if the heart of the world had stopped beating.

'What can you hear?' Jannet asked.

Gioga stared at her. 'Nothing, Mam.'

'Not the sea?'

Gioga shook her head, too upset now to speak.

'You're a good girl. You'll be all right.' Jannet pressed the child's hand in her own. 'It's for your own good. I promise you.'

They found Madelaine and Rab in a barn, sorting out wool for spinning. Gioga stood apart, watching Jannet as she talked to them, saw them all glancing towards her, and hung her head. Madelaine came back with Jannet, wiping oil from her big red hands, peering down at Gioga with kind eyes. 'You coming to help me and Rab?' she smiled, cocking her head to one side. Gioga said nothing.

'I'll go now,' Jannet said quickly. 'If I don't get back to the old man before dark I'll be wandering all night.'

Gioga clung to her, afraid and bewildered, not understanding what she had done to be sent away like this.

'Now, please don't do that. There's a good girl,' Jannet begged her, trying to hide her own distress. 'It's only for a little while, and then you can come home again. We'll come and see you very soon.'

'And Harris?'

'Yes, Harris too.'

'I told him I'd bring him something from Mainland.'

'I've seen to that. The old woman we stayed with last night gave me a hat she'd just knitted for her grandson. Don't you think this will look fine on Harris's head?'

It cheered Gioga up, but not much. It wasn't as good as a fiddle. Madelaine watched from her barn and tutted. 'It's an uncanny matter!' she whispered to her husband. 'Apparently the bairn has to be kept from the sea, as it makes her ill! Did you ever hear anything like it? It's uncanny, that is.'

Gioga stood forlornly at the door of the house until long after Jannet had disappeared. She felt sure that she would never see her again. Madelaine called her indoors, but still she stood, gazing down the valley of silence. She had never known such stillness. No breath of wind, no creak of grass, no dribble of water. Nothing but the hoarse rasping of ravens on the red-berried thorn.

9
The Third Visit

It was the ninth day of the highest tide of the year. The sea lapped around Eilean's boat, and nearly to the very door of Jannet's house. The sheep had been moved to the walled fields, and still the tide surged at the stones. The wind brought hail. Frost glittered on the grass.

Jannet sat in the house that day, listening to the rush of the tide, and knew that Hill Marliner would return. Her eyes rested on something hanging by the door and moved away again. She wouldn't allow herself to look at it.

She took up her knitting and glanced again at the

thing by the door. It was Munroe's, not hers. It was nothing to do with her. She had no idea how to use it. She had never been able to bring herself to touch it, such a cold, merciless thing. She couldn't bear to look any longer.

Restless, she went to the door. The sky and the sea were one drab colour. The rocks looked like the pods of whales that passed by the islands, jetting fountains of spume. A movement in the bay made her glance back again. There was the stranger, coming towards her.

Jannet turned round quickly, wanting to get away from him, but there rose up out of the sea such a strange wild singing that she was stopped in her tracks. The cry seemed to come from the air and the earth, from every rock and stone, every blade of grass and pebble, every grain of sand.

'Go away!' she shouted. 'She's not here.'

'Then bring her to me,' Hill Marliner said. 'I'll not be leaving without her this time.'

Jannet ran into the house. The thing by the door gleamed in the firelight: Munroe's hunting gun.

In a frenzy that was close to madness Jannet reached out for it. She had watched Munroe clean and load it for hunting, but she had never touched it herself. Now, with that chanting raging in her head, and not knowing what to do with herself for fear, she took hold of the gun and raised it and fired it. And the first shot struck home and the singing stopped.

Jannet closed the door and leaned against it, her hands over her face.

'What have I done?' she whispered.

She knew Munroe would not come home before dark. She began to sob with fear for what he would find and what he might say. She tried to calm herself with busyness, not daring to leave the house or even go to the door. When Munroe came in and stood in the blackness behind her she did not turn round. He came up to her and put his hand on her arm and she stopped what she was doing and made herself look at him.

'Come outside, will you,' he said. 'There's something you should see.'

He drew her out, and in the half-light of a moon that swung like a lantern between clouds Jannet saw two figures on the wet shingle. One was Eilean, crouched on her knees and moaning. The other was stretched out and still and colder than sleep. There was blood on the ground from a wound in his side. And it was no man, but a seal.

10

The Revenge

At that moment there rose from the sea such a wailing of grief that Jannet's blood ran cold to hear it. She could not bring herself to approach the seal that was lying on the ground, but Munroe led her up to it.

She could see that his flippers were like hands, that his fingers had their nails on them still, and that his open staring eyes had a look in them of horror and pain.

'Why did you do this?' asked Munroe. 'The Jaffreys do not kill seals.'

'She did it to save the child,' said Eilean, standing

up and shaking wet sand from her skirt and her shawl. 'And Hill Marliner knew that she would do it. All the seals knew.'

From where they were standing they could see the seals clambering up on to the sands and the rocks, rippling towards them, their mouths wide open as they gave out their howls of sorrow.

'I'm afraid,' said Jannet.

'We'll go back into the house and see what we must do,' her husband told her.

He closed and bolted the door against the terrible sound that they could hear from the sea. He lifted peats on to the fire and lit a lantern from the flames. Then he told Jannet about the night he had found Gioga in the rock pool among the skerries; how, when he lifted her out of the water, a fur skin slipped away from her, and how he let the skin drown.

'What does that mean?' she asked, hardly daring to look at him.

'You know as well as I what that means. Gioga is not one of us, but one of them. She's a child of the sea.'

'Will she ever go back to them?'

'Not without her skin. She can't. She has to stay with us. No matter how many times the seal people had come for her, she could never return with them. She was quite safe, you see. You had no need to do what you did.'

Wind slammed against the door, then dipped into silence. The beasts lowed in their straw.

'Why didn't you tell me about the seal skin?'

'Why didn't you tell me about Hill Marliner?' he asked.

The husband and wife stared at each other, aware of their own guilt and ashamed of it.

'What will happen now?' asked Jannet.

'We will see,' Munroe said. 'When dawn comes, I think we will see.'

When dawn came they went down with the other crofters to see the damage that had been done in the night. The salmon nets had been torn down, whole salmon lay half-eaten and spoiled on the pebbles, the fishing boats had been pushed into the sea and were drifting away or smashed against the rocks, nets had been trailed and broken into shreds. Hill Marliner's body had been dragged back into the sea, leaving behind it a trail of blood that would never be washed away.

The crofters stood in silent groups on the shore, aghast at the havoc the seals had wreaked.

'That's our livelihood done away with,' said Morag's husband.

But even more terrible than the wreckage all around them, was the incessant wailing and moaning of the seals. All day and all night the chorus could be heard. And then it was gone. The seals had left Hamna Voe.

11
Old Voices Tell Tales

From that time there was no holding back the fury of the sea. The tides were high and wild, crashing against the cliffs and sending white plumes into the sky. Gulls were blown backwards and forwards like white rags of cloth. Their cries were lost. The heather thatches were lifted from the roofs of the crofts and had to be weighted down with nets hung with stones. Water coursed over the fields and ruined the winter crops.

Months went by. The tides were relentless, sweeping across the island, cutting off the north from the south. Ice fringed the shores. Hail lashed the earth. At the end of the sunless winter the people of the crofts came together in Munroe's house to see what could be done.

'We are prisoners on this island,' said old Mary, who had never left it in her life.

'Even if the seas calmed down, and we made more boats, we are finished,' said Morag's husband. 'There are no fish in that sea. They've left us.'

'This is all because of the killing of the seal,' said Grandfather Jaffrey, and Mary agreed with him.

'It was my own father who put a stop to the killing of seals in our family,' she said, 'after a seal saved his life.'

There was flame-light on the faces of the people in the room, and the only voice for a time was the flickering tongue of the fire, as people thought their thoughts and said nothing.

'What was that story?' Harris asked. He was the youngest on the island since Gioga had gone. He did the work of the men, trying to save what he could from the sodden earth, and to pluck out what little the sea left behind in pools. But he was still a child, lonely for the company of other children.

'It was my father whose boat was wrecked on one of the rocks, far out, when the storm was so wild that none of the others could reach him,' Mary went on.

'Or would want to,' put in old Grandfather Jaffrey. 'Let the sea take. We're not to interfere with that.'

'And my father was alone on the rock.' There were shadows under Mary's eyes and cheekbones. Her hands worked at her knitting, though she never glanced down at it. 'And he thought he would never reach home again, and there was my mother lamenting in the house for him, seeing the tide like this. She was in despair for herself and our family. And a seal swam up to my father and said, "You will not be happy out here on the rocks that were meant for the seals."'

'He would be lonely there, wouldn't he?' said Harris.

Mary nodded, not looking at him, daydreams in her milky eyes. 'And my father said, "Yes." "Ah," the seal went on, "but the seals that have lost their skins will always be lonely on land, and can never return to sea without them. I have lost my son in this way. He is a man on the land since you've taken his skin." And my father went cold in his heart because he'd been sealing all that week and had seal skins stretched on the floor of his home. "I will

94

bring you to land," said the seal, "if you'll bring me the skins you've taken. Climb on my back."'

'He'd be frightened of slipping off her back into the sea,' said Harris.

'He was afraid, but she let him cut notches in her skin for his hands and his feet to fit into. He clung to her and over the waves they came and landed on shore. He ran to his croft, our croft on the end of the island, gathered up the seal skins in his arms and flung them into the sea. He heard the seals singing that night as he'd never heard them before. He never killed seals again.'

'I heard he was carried home safe on a seal's back,' said Morag. 'I never heard about him giving back the skins before.'

'It's true all the same,' said Mary, her bright self again.

'I don't know how you could speak to seals and understand their voices,' Morag went on. 'I never heard of that, either.'

'Eilean knows,' said Harris, and they all turned to the crab-woman who was sitting silent and apart at the far end of the room where the animals slept.

'I know,' Eilean said, 'and I know there is only one way to cure their anger. And it is for you to do.'

She nodded at Munroe and Jannet. 'You must bring your daughter home.'

Jannet and Munroe kept silent. They knew this too, in their hearts, but had never spoken the thought to each other.

Morag laughed in her sharp, rough way. It wasn't a laugh at all. 'Bring her home,' she scorned, 'and she on Mainland! How would anyone cross a sea like this? We've only one boat left between us, and that would be smashed to pieces.'

'Munroe must go for her all the same,' said Eilean, 'and I will go with him.'

'Can I go?' asked Harris. 'I want to see Gioga. I want to bring her back!'

'No, you shan't go,' said Morag. 'You would be drowned out there, on a sea like that.'

'The boy will be safe enough.' Eilean turned to go away from the room, and as she did so, she looked quickly at Harris. She said nothing, but the words in her eyes told him to follow her.

The adults were talking again amongst themselves. Tam had brought out his fiddle and was playing a soft lament, and it was a soothing thing for Harris to hear as he slipped out into the night and made his way down towards Eilean's boat house. Black waves churned against the rocks. Hail scraped his cheeks like gravel. He could hardly stand upright in the wind.

He paused for a moment outside Eilean's door, scared, not understanding why he'd been drawn to follow her like that. She called him inside.

'I have something to give you,' she said, 'and something to tell you, and something to show you. You must keep all these things secret in your heart until the time comes.'

Harris nodded and edged closer to where she was sitting, hunched on a stool by the stone hearth of her fire.

'This is what I have to give you,' she said. She reached down and held towards him a gleaming harpoon. 'This was my father's,' she told him. 'From the days when he roamed the seas in search of whales and seals to kill. I want you to have it now.'

He backed away, his hands behind him, shaking his head. His cheeks were smudged with the black smoke from the fire and wet from the drizzle and sleet on the air outside. He was shivering.

'I see you're a child yet,' Eilean said. 'But before you are a man you will have need of this. Take it. Without its help you cannot bring Gioga home.'

This time he took it from her. His hands were trembling.

'Before you go back to your croft tonight you must take the harpoon and lay it in the boat that we will be travelling in tomorrow. Cover it with sacking so that it will not be seen. Now,' she went on, 'you have fed on stories tonight, but I have one more to tell you. Sit.'

He squatted on his haunches.

'It's a story about a woman who lived on land but did not belong to it,' Eilean said quietly. 'Have you heard of such a woman?'

'She would be a selkie,' said Harris. His throat was dry and aching with tiredness. The peat smoke stung his eyes. He wanted to sleep. While Eilean told the story he closed his eyes and let the quiet chant of her voice and the purr of the flames wash over him, until he did not know whether it was a story he was hearing or a dream.

He was roused at last by the sound of Eilean's feet padding across the floor. She dipped a brand into the fire and set it alight.

'Now come with me,' she said, 'and see what I have to show you.'

He followed her outside to a huddle of rocks just behind her boat house. He clambered up after her. Eilean set down the brand so its reflection glittered in a pool, drew back her shawls to bare her arms, and plunged her hands into the water. She drew something out and stretched it across the rocks between them, and then held up the brand so that he could see it clearly.

'This belongs to the girl,' she whispered. 'Do you know what it is?'

'I do.' Harris nodded. He ached with dread.

'Go back to your croft now,' Eilean told him. 'You need your sleep and your strength for tomorrow. And when you see Gioga tell her all these things. And this: she will weep seven tears into the ocean.'

The next day they set off. All the crofters were down on the beach to watch, clinging to each other against the batterings of the wind. The men helped to lift the boulders that were holding down the last boat, and to push it from its stone nest into the sea. Munroe took hold of the oars, not looking at Jannet, sure that this time the sea would claim him. Harris crouched down like a rabbit in a hole, red hair lashing his eyes and the flung sand stinging his cheeks. Eilean sat hunched with her shawls around her. Spray showered them as they lumbered out into the bay.

As soon as they rounded the rocks and had lost

sight of the island, Eilean stood up in the boat. Harris was bailing out water as fast as he could. Waves slammed across them.

'Now save us if you can!' Munroe shouted to Eilean. His words blew away from him like birds.

'I will raise three waves that are higher than man has ever seen before,' said Eilean. 'The first will be of milk. The second will be of tears. The third will be of blood. Turn your boat straight into the heart of each of these waves, and when the third wave comes, the wave of blood, you, Harris, must throw the harpoon into it. And I will be in that wave. The harpoon will pierce me. That is the only way you will reach land alive.'

Before they had time to take in her words a huge swell came towards them, a massive mountain of a wave that was as white as milk.

Munroe pulled back with one oar and swung the boat nose-first into the heart of the wave. The boat came through it, but riding instantly behind the first came the even higher wave, clear as ice.

Again he swung the nose of the boat into the wave and again they came through it, and instantly behind it was an even higher wave that was as red as blood.

Harris heard a voice screaming at him, 'Now!'

He picked up the harpoon from the bottom of the boat and, with all his might, flung it into the centre of the wave. It parted on each side of them. The sea paused, and hushed down into stillness. There was no sign of Eilean in the boat, or in the sea around them. And the tempests of winter were gone.

12

Out of the Valley

Madelaine and her husband Rab had taken in Gioga because she was Jannet's child. They looked after her as well as they could, but they never came to understand her. To them she was a sullen moping child, unwilling to say anything to them or answer them when they spoke to her. She did as she was told and helped Madelaine with her spinning, or helped Rab to round up the ponies. She dug the potatoes and threw grain to the hens. But she kept her head down low all the time.

'She's a strange child,' said Madelaine to her husband one day when they were working side by side in the croft. 'Have you noticed that she never looks at us at all?'

'She's like a little ghost,' her husband agreed. 'I think she's grieving.'

'For her mother and father?'

'For something. She stays awake all night, grieving.'

Gioga never seemed to sleep. Night after night they found her standing at the door or the window, wide-eyed, shivering with cold. Some nights she would be pacing about the floor or sitting upright in the straw in the little half-loft which was hers to sleep in, staring in front of her, her fists tight in her lap.

'Poor thing,' said Madelaine. 'I wish Jannet would come for her. I don't know what to do with the child.'

It was deep winter. In the dark valley ice glittered on every leaf and blade of grass. Nothing moved across the frozen earth. The shoulders of the mountains were deep in snow. All was still and silent, and yet deep inside herself Gioga listened to the slow and steady lapping of a tide that was the pulsing of her own blood. It was the only thing that comforted her.

At last the dark days began to lighten and the ice

began to melt. Snow shrank to the edges of the fields. Water coursed down the mountain sides into the valley. The flowers of spring began to open up.

Madelaine took Gioga outside to see how the sunshine was lighting up the valley. She saw how thin and pale the child had grown, how dark her eyes were from weeks and weeks of not sleeping. 'Are you ill?' she asked her.

Gioga bent down to look at the frail snowdrops in the grass. They reminded her of speckles of foam on the sand.

'I wish you'd say something,' said Madelaine. She went in to speak to her husband, her round face puckered. 'I know she's my cousin's own child, but I can't seem to get close to her,' she said. 'I think she should go home.'

'They said the sea was making her ill,' he reminded her.

She shook her head. Their own children were grown up now, with families themselves. They had never had trouble like this with any of them. 'It seems more like it's being away from the sea that's ailing her. I don't know what to do.'

'Take her home.' He spread out his hands as if his words were a gift. 'It's simple, Madelaine.'

When they came out again they were carrying Gioga's clothes in a bundle.

'I can't bear to see you like this any longer,' Madelaine said to Gioga. Her husband whistled a pony and lifted Gioga on to its back.

'But where are we going?' Gioga asked.

'Away.'

For the first time since they'd met her, Gioga smiled. 'Away? To the sea?'

Madelaine exchanged looks with her husband. 'Aye, maybe,' said Madelaine. 'Away to the sea.'

Harris and Munroe had brought their boat in smoothly to Mainland. The landing stage was deserted, so there was no one to guide them. They walked along the track that Jannet had taken all those months ago with Gioga, repeating to each other the directions she had given them to the house of the old couple who had given her shelter. They would tell them how to find Madelaine and Rab, Jannet promised. It was nearly the end of the day when they reached the old people's house. They knocked, but there was silence.

Munroe pushed open the door to find the house empty, a cold hearth and no food in the larder, no geese or hens around the place, no crops in the field.

'Well, they've died, or been moved on by the laird,' said Munroe. 'What do we do now? We've no idea where to go.'

They spent the night there for shelter and set off again soon after dawn. The task seemed hopeless. There were so many valleys; it was impossible to know which way to turn.

'I think we should go back,' said Munroe.

'But we can't go home without Gioga,' Harris urged.

It wasn't until the end of the second day of walking that they saw in the distance a dusty track, a man and a woman leading a child on a pony.

'It's Gioga,' said Harris. 'I know it is.' He began to run, pulling off his knitted hat and waving his arms in the air. Munroe loped behind, clumsy on his aching feet.

'Harris!' Gioga nearly fell off the pony's back in her eagerness to be on the ground and racing to him. 'I never thought I'd see you again.'

'It's high time you came,' Madelaine called out to Munroe. 'She's sick for home, this child.'

Gioga would not look at Munroe. He put both his hands on her shoulders and tried to make her smile at him. He was shocked by the change in her.

'I'm sorry this happened to you.' He tried to tell

her about the wild seas that had been beating round the island for months. 'No one could come for you.'

'Are we really going home?' she asked him. 'How long will it take? Can we go now?'

'It's a long way yet,' Madelaine told her. 'You'll need another full day.' She took them to a friend's house where they could stay the night, and went on home, relieved to be rid of the strange child at last. Munroe and Harris fell straight into a snoring sleep. They were weary with so much walking. Gioga lay with her eyes wide open, listening. She hadn't slept for months.

The next day she woke them as soon as the sun was up and ran ahead of them. The track was taking them up a steep hill, and as soon as she reached the top, there was the sea, the long shimmering stretch of it on the horizon.

'I can hear the sea,' Gioga shouted.

Harris panted after her. 'Not yet,' he gasped. 'You can hardly see it yet.'

But Gioga could hear its distant roar, the roll of it round her island, every splash and ripple it made in her bay.

The island was hidden in spindrift, but as they approached the mist cleared. There was a golden light across the slopes and the sand was as red as wine. Sheep dotted the pale green fringe of grass. Blue peat smoke drifted above the houses.

On the shore were the people of the island, come to welcome Gioga. Mary and Margaret and Grandfather Jaffray were like three fence posts leaning towards each other, propping each other up, shouting out greetings. And in front of them stood Jannet, holding out her arms to her.

It was a wonderful homecoming. Everyone marvelled at the calm sea and the placid sky. Nobody mentioned how pale Gioga looked. They all went back to the house together and Jannet stirred the peats to make the flames burst and dance. Morag had seen to the cheese scones and tarts, the rhubarb punch, kept ready for feasts. Tam brought out his fiddle and played the jigs and airs that Gioga remembered best, and late in the day Harris showed her the fiddle that Grandfather Jaffray had carved for him and that he had learned to play. He and Tam stood together, fiddles tucked under their chins, feet slightly apart. The two bows swung in unison, fingers danced on the strings, toes tapped. Harris frowned in concentration, but now and again he glanced over to Gioga to see if she liked what he was doing, and returned her smile.

When the visitors had all left Jannet took Gioga to her sleeping-place and sat by her.

'I promised you would come home again, didn't I? How I wish we had been able to send for you before now.'

Someone would have to tell the child about Hill Marliner, and about Eilean, washed away in the wave of blood, but not yet. She didn't want anything to spoil the homecoming.

'Is this the end of the story?' Munroe asked, thinking Gioga was asleep at last.

Jannet frowned. 'When Gioga is happy, I'll be happy,' she said.

Gioga had closed her eyes, pretending to sleep. She was listening to the way the waves washed over the rocks and trickled down through all the grains of sand. She was not home yet.

13

The Seven Tears

'Why would I weep seven tears into the ocean?'
Gioga asked.

Harris shrugged. They were sitting outside
Eilean's boat house, now wrecked by the winter
storms. He told her then of the seal that had been
found outside Jannet's house, with a gun wound in
its side, and how it had disappeared the next day.

'And since that day there have been no seals in
Hamna Voe or anywhere around the island.
They've gone.'

While Gioga was listening to this story there was
a stillness about her as if she might never breathe

again. Harris couldn't look at her; there was much more to tell her. He would wait for her to speak.

'I want to know now where Eilean is,' Gioga said at last.

He told her about the night when Eilean had given him her father's harpoon, and of the riding across a sea that was as wild as a field of ponies, and of the wave of milk, and the wave of tears, and of the wave of blood. He told her that it was he himself who had thrown the harpoon.

'But it was Eilean who told me to do it,' he said.

'Then it must have been right,' Gioga answered. 'You calmed the sea so I could come home again. But it's not the same if the seals have gone.'

'They brought terrible storms. Everyone thinks it was the seals who made the storms.'

Away on the fields the corn shoots were tiny green buds. A lapwing creaked on the fence. Flowers beaded the slopes of the hills, and the turquoise sea shimmered in sunlight. It was hard to remember the battering of hail and wind, and the towering grey seas of winter.

'But it's true,' Harris said. 'It's not the same without them. I miss them too.' He made a funny barking noise in the back of his throat.

'And I miss Eilean too.'

'She said I have to tell you something and show you something,' Harris said, remembering his task and his promise.

'Is it about the selkies?'

'Eilean told me this story for you.' He frowned, trying to remember the exact words Eilean o da Freya had used that night, when she had told him the tale in his half-asleep state by the fire. He could hear her voice now, in his head, and the way she had crooned on the words.

'A long time ago a man was walking by the sea and came across some people dancing. It seemed to him that they were dancing round their shadows that lay still in the moonlight. And when they saw him, the dancing people picked up their shadows and flung them across their shoulders, and he saw that they were seals putting back their seal skins. They ran into the sea, but as they were running the man picked up one of the seal skins and hid it behind a rock. And a girl ran from rock to rock, looking for her seal skin, and at last, seeing him, came crying to him, asking if he had seen a grey cloak on the sand. And he told her he hadn't. He put his own coat around her and hid the skin from her. He took her home with him. And for a long time the girl wept bitterly to go back to the sea, but she could never return without her skin.'

'But how could he be so cruel?' Gioga said. 'To keep it from her?'

'Eilean said it was because he loved her. He married her and they had children. Many years later, when the children were playing, one of them found the skin. He didn't know what it was, and he took it to his mother and showed it to her. She recognized it at once. Her heart was torn in two, because she loved her husband and she loved her children, but now she had her skin she knew she could return to the sea.'

'And did she?' asked Gioga.

Harris nodded.

'Then the story had a happy ending.'

'I don't think so,' said Harris.

'You said you had something to show me.'

'I promised Eilean I would show you,' Harris said, 'but I don't want to. I know what it is, but I don't understand why I have to show it to you.' But even as he said it, he did understand.

He took her up to the rocks behind the shattered boat house. There, in their shelter, was a deep pool. He put his hands in, just as he had seen Eilean do that night, and he brought out the silvery seal skin and placed it on the rocks beside Gioga. Then he turned and ran for home.

Gioga picked up the skin, wondering. It was grey and smooth. She held it against her cheek and recognized its warmth. She pressed her face in it and knew its smell from long ago. She knew that it was her own.

She went back down to the sea and sat on one of the rocks with the skin in her arms. Her mind was a spin of questions. She thought about Hill Marliner, the strange visitor. She knew he was the seal-man that Jannet had shot. She thought about Eilean o da Freya, and of how she had given herself to the sea. She thought of Jannet and Munroe, who loved her, and how they had sent her away to save her. She thought of the seals that had left Hamna Voe. She wept for these seven things.

'Gioga!' she heard someone cry. 'Gioga! Come home!' The cry was a song that came from below the sea, and she knew the language at last. Joy rippled through her, sadness and longing. All around her the waters glinted with lights, shapes shifted, green below green rose up from the echoing sea-floor, from the shell-beds and winnowing weed-grass, from fathoms-deep hiding. 'Gioga!' came the song. 'Come home!'

In their croft Munroe and Jannet had heard the cry too. They came to the door of their house and stood together, looking across the bay of Hamna Voe. 'They have come,' said Jannet. 'Now is the end of the story.' She lifted her hand, a white banner, a wave of farewell.

Gioga slipped the seal skin over her shoulders, wrapped it around herself like a cloak, and shimmered into the sea. A circle of ripples spiralled out wide and deep and splintered into the sunlight. Then all was still.

Author's Note

Some of the stories woven into *Daughter of the Sea* are based on ancient tales from Iceland, Scotland and Ireland.